CUPCAKES AND CATASTROPHE

A BELLE HARBOR COZY MYSTERY (BOOK 1)

SUE HOLLOWELL

Cupcakes and Catastrophe

Cover by: Donna L. Rogers - DLR Cover Designs

Editing by: Tiffany White at Writers Untapped

CONTENTS

1. CHAPTER ONE   1

2. CHAPTER TWO   6

3. CHAPTER THREE   11

4. CHAPTER FOUR   16

5. CHAPTER FIVE   22

6. CHAPTER SIX   27

7. CHAPTER SEVEN   32

8. CHAPTER EIGHT   37

9. CHAPTER NINE   42

10. CHAPTER TEN   47

11. CHAPTER ELEVEN   52

12. CHAPTER TWELVE   57

13. CHAPTER THIRTEEN   62

14. CHAPTER FOURTEEN   66

15. CHAPTER FIFTEEN   71

What's Next? Muffins and Misdeeds   75

Sneak Peek of Muffins and Misdeeds   76

What's After Muffins and Misdeeds?   78

More From Sue Hollowell   80

Cream-filled Cupcakes Recipe   83

About The Author   85

CHAPTER ONE

"Uncle Jack, you don't have to do that. Why don't you sit and rest a bit?" My dear uncle had been working nonstop ever since I had agreed to move to Belle Harbor. I wasn't so sure about the arrangement, but I was ready for a big change in my life. And I couldn't get a much bigger change than leaving the cold East Coast city of Boston, Massachusetts, and leaping across the country to the small, sunny beach town of Belle Harbor. In some ways, it was an easy transition. Who could argue with the weather? And Uncle Jack was one of my favorite people on the planet. The scariest part was finally pursuing my dream of opening a bakery, just like my Grandma Luna had done.

"Don't be silly, Tilly," Uncle Jack said. "Hey, I made a rhyme."

I rolled my eyes. Truthfully, Uncle Jack's organization system left a lot to be desired. He ran the Checkered Past Antique shop right on the boardwalk at Belle Harbor. I couldn't see how he had an inkling of what was in the store. From my vantage point, it was a hodgepodge of junk. A set of six crystal wine glasses sat next to a statue of an old sea mariner holding binoculars, next to a two-foot-tall silver-stemmed bowl holding what looked like fake dill pickles. Somehow, he and his brother had made it work for decades.

"I can't thank you enough, Unkie. You really are making my dream come true." I strolled through the aisles of treasures, surveying how I might help him better arrange the pieces for sale. I made mental notes, not wanting to upset the apple cart on my first official day. I stopped and observed him furiously working in the corner he had cleared out to make room for my very first bakeshop. Moving items out of the space for my supplies created even bigger piles of antiques. "You really should let me help you."

He lifted his head from his focus at the work counter he had set up for my baking. "Oh, Til." His voiced cracked. He stepped toward me and held out his hand. "I would do anything for you."

Somehow, he had gotten a smudge of flour on his face. I reached up and wiped it away. He tilted his head and smiled warmly. We both returned to the baking corner. He had fully equipped me with a little kitchen to begin my new life as a baker. The area had an oven, sink, cabinets, and counters for supplies and tools. The only thing was... his system for setting it up looked exactly the same as his antique store. I would later find a way to hopefully, without his noticing, shift things around to be more usable for my purposes.

"OK, let's sit for a bit," he said. I followed him to the side of the cash register, where we each plopped into an Elizabethan-style wooden chair. I felt like we were waiting for the jester to arrive and perform for us. Uncle Jack was a spry seventy-year-old man with vigor for life. I knew my move here would inject all kinds of adventure into my life. I just wasn't sure what it would be. He had lost a bit of his step ever since his brother, and partner in the store, had passed away. Those two together caused a lot of mischief, according to my mom. But I had only ever seen them as a hoot while I was growing up.

Mom and Dad never knew what to do with me, so they shipped me off every summer to stay with Jack and Frank. Little did they know, it only emboldened my creative side. I was about as far as you could get from the stodgy professions of my parents.

I looked at him and reached over to grab his hand. It was well worn from a life of physical labor. My uncle was never one to shy away from hard work. His balding head and trim white beard framed his warm brown eyes. That man really would do anything for his friends and family.

"I'm thinking I'll name the bakery Luna's Bakeshop. What do you think?"

He rested his head against the tall back of the chair, closed his eyes, and smiled. "She would be so pleased you're following in her footsteps." Grandma Luna was as much of a kook as my uncles. I couldn't figure out how in a million years my mom turned out the way she did. Perhaps a reverse rebellion from a wild and crazy mother of her own. He turned and looked at me. "You look like her too. In her day, she wouldn't have dyed her hair blue like you have. But everything else? The spitting image."

That couldn't have been a higher compliment. I would take that as a sign I was on the right track for my new life. "So I'm planning to make Grandma's signature cream-filled cupcakes for my inaugural recipe."

Uncle Jack shook his head. "Tilly, you're going to be a hit in this town. They'll be lining up out the door. And I don't mean just customers."

I stood, turned, and pointed a finger at him. "Don't you dare fix me up. I just got out of a relationship, and I'm nowhere near ready for another. I'm going to focus on building my business and just enjoying myself for a change." I moved to a nearby table, piled high with antiques, and shifted a few things around to busy myself. Truthfully, I wanted to hide from life in my bakery. The ink hadn't even dried on my divorce papers. Any thoughts of that life, three thousand miles away, hurt my heart. And if I let my mind go there, it quickly became a downward spiral. In time I would process it. But not today.

Uncle Jack pushed himself out of the chair. I heard a couple of cracks in the quiet store, probably both from his knees and the old furniture. He steadied himself and said, "Let's step outside and see what's going on with the kite festival. I could use some warmth in these old bones."

I looked around. "But who's going to watch the store?"

He waved his arm around the space. "Everyone's at the kite festival. And besides, we'll only go far enough so that we can still see if someone comes in."

That was something else I would have to get used to. In the big city, if you left your business unattended, you would certainly come back to looters. OK, maybe not that bad, but why take a chance?

We stepped through the doorway to the bright sun and warmth. I stopped, closed my eyes, and lifted my face, taking in a deep breath. I could easily get used to this weather.

With my move to the beach, I had needed to get a whole new wardrobe. I took pleasure in donating my winter woolies and buying some things that more closely fit my personality. No more prim and proper styles; now I was all into preppy, casual, beach fun.

Along with getting my bobbed hair colored to match the ocean, I purchased several pairs of Converse shoes in just about every color and style to match a mood. Today's pair matched the blues and greens of the sea. Of course, I stocked up on T-shirts, and as Grandma Luna would call them, pedal pushers. In modern lingo, capris. Stepping into that outfit this morning and doing a once-over in the full-length mirror made me feel like I was one step further along my journey to a new life. And to spend time with Uncle Jack, who I expected to be my partner-in-crime was a dream come true.

CHAPTER TWO

"Why don't we just sit here so we can stay close in case someone wants to buy something?" I gestured to the bench up against the outer wall of the antique shop. I wasn't convinced it was safe to venture very far. Though, if someone did steal something, it might just make a bit more room to organize what remained.

Uncle Jack turned to look at me. "Tilly, don't be a worry wart. I've been doing this a long time. It'll be fine. Live a little, darlin'." He strolled out toward the beach.

I looked both ways, didn't see any sketchy characters, and followed his path. I crossed the boardwalk that separated our shops from the greater part of the beach. The official portion of the kite competition was on a break. Amateurs attempted to hoist their kites into the air. I stopped again, breathed in deep, and gazed up and down the beach. Kites of all styles were in flight. I jogged to catch up with my uncle. Beach living must have provided him ample opportunity to keep in shape. By the time I reached him, I had to stop and catch my breath. "Uncle Jack," I said, bent over, wheezing.

He turned and came back to my side. "Oh, girl. Soon you'll have the stamina of a seventy-year-old." He rocked his head back in laughter. "Isn't this beautiful?" He swept his arm around. I wasn't sure what he referred to, but everything as far as I could see was indeed breathtaking. The blue-green ocean sparkled with the sun glinting off the water. The warmth permeated to my bones, like a blanket hugging me. Kids squealed, enjoying family time in their little huddles up and down the beach while watching the kite competition.

I stood and held out my hand to him. "This is amazing. What a fun event."

Even though I had lived in Boston, which had access to multiple beaches, neither my parents nor my ex had any interest in visiting and enjoying the ocean. It was all work and no play. When I did have a moment to myself, I made a beeline to the coast. It refreshed my soul like nothing else. The expanse of the water, sky, and sand gave me peace. It fueled my creativity—the little time I had to spend on it. My bookkeeping job helped pay the bills, but it did nothing to serve my passion. I longed to follow in Grandma Luna's footsteps and own my own bakery. I had to pinch myself to make sure my current reality wasn't a dream.

I didn't have much time with her, but when Grandma Luna and I were together, I felt like we were kindred spirits. My parents referred to her derisively as a hippie that never grew up. Whatever she was, she always seemed incredibly joyful with life. I desperately longed for that. It wasn't until after a lot of conversations that finally my ex agreed to culinary school. I remember the day vividly. A huge rock in my throat almost kept me from speaking my mind. I had visited Grandma in the hospital as she lay dying. Her body was wearing out. She took my hand, looked deeply into my eyes, and urged me to follow my passion. She had squeezed my hand for emphasis, and at that moment some sort of boldness overcame me like never before.

With my borrowed confidence from my grandma, I told my ex I would be attending culinary school. He blinked and took a step back. I stood with my hands on my hips like Wonder Woman, not willing to budge an inch. This was happening. I had no way of knowing it would also lead to the end of my marriage.

I had gathered my breath sufficiently to continue walking along the beach.

"This is day two. Every year there's a handful of the most competitive fliers who duke it out. Looks like the perennial favorite is in third place." Uncle Jack gestured to a leader board that listed last names in rank order. At the top was Burkhart followed by Simon, then Powell. "That's not going to sit well with Maverick. I know he's been tuning up his gear for quite some time. He doesn't like to lose."

I shaded my eyes and looked at Uncle Jack. "You know him?"

"Oh, yeah. I know most everyone in town." We continued roaming around the sand.

I stopped. "Don't you think we should return to the store?" I turned to look back and could barely see the door of the antique shop. It didn't appear anyone was near, so maybe he was right. We were safe for a short period of time.

"OK. If it'll make you feel better, big-city girl." He chuckled. "I'm hopeful you'll shed your stress and join me in chill town."

"Me too," I said. We retraced our steps back to the store. "Uncle Jack, can you slow down just a bit?" I stopped. How was that man so fit?

He came back to where I stood. "It's settled. I'm going to buy you a moped. You'll need that anyway when you start delivering all of your wares."

I shook my head and resumed walking, trying to set the pace. "You don't have to do that."

He jetted out front of me, and I did my best to keep up. At this rate, I would need a nap when we got back. "I insist. Plus, I know the gal who runs the shop. She'll give me a good deal."

I attempted to half-jog, hoping I wouldn't collapse right there and end my new life just as it was getting started. "Well, I'll pay you back. Every penny. I counted on other people my entire life. And now I'm counting on myself."

Uncle Jack abruptly stopped and pointed a finger at me. "I don't want to hear any more of that talk, missy. You are an incredible woman. We each take our own path. You've learned a lot that you can now apply to this new season. But it wasn't for naught."

He was right. My journey brought me to this point, so it couldn't have been all bad. And I had my very own amateur therapist to keep me grounded. What an incredible first day on my new odyssey. I looked forward to getting back to my little corner kitchen and starting on those cupcakes.

I could easily see the door to the shop now and my anxiety decreased a bit. I only hoped we weren't ripped off during our little jaunt down the beach.

Uncle Jack turned to me and said, "See? Everything's fine." He grinned and displayed those hard-earned laugh lines. I smiled. Eventually I would adjust. How could you not?

We both whipped our heads around as a blood-curdling scream emanated from the direction of the shop. Maybe I spoke too soon? Like a man fifty years his junior, my uncle sped off toward the horrific sound. I followed as closely as possible but was unable to keep up. As we got closer, it became clear the shriek was from the vacant shop next to Checkered Past Antiques. We both entered through the propped-open door.

Standing about six feet inside with her hand over her mouth was an elderly woman. Her eyes were as large as plates. Uncle Jack and I both followed her gaze to see a dead body on the floor in the middle of the room. She shook her head, unable to speak.

Uncle Jack took a step closer. I grabbed his arm. He turned and said, "That's Cal. One of the kite competition judges. He's been strangled."

CHAPTER THREE

A whimper came from the woman to our side. I judged her to be about the same age as my uncle. She looked like she was attending a formal tea party. A string of pearls topped her floral, sleeveless dress. A small straw hat covered her pixie silver haircut. A bold, dark set of eyeglasses sat atop her nose. She lowered her chin and peered over the top of the glasses.

"Why is he here?" She pointed at the body, averting her eyes. "This is my building."

Uncle Jack and I looked at each other and shrugged. "The kite competition judges were using this space. I didn't know anyone owned this," Uncle Jack said.

The lady stepped away from the body and angled herself toward the door. With her hand shielding her eyes, she said, "You need to get him out of here." She took two more steps toward the door, her heels clopping loudly throughout the empty room.

I peeked at the body and saw a man younger than Uncle Jack laying on his side like he was taking a nap. The table where the judges sat to perform the scoring was on its side. The three metal folding chairs were haphazardly strewn away from the table, like someone had scooted them out before turning the table over.

The man wore board shorts, flip flops, and a black- and white-striped referee shirt. The scoring pages were strewn across the floor. The easel and chart paper with scores lay on its side. The list and order of names mirrored those on the chart at the beach. Who would do this? I imagined the competition was serious, but enough to take out a judge who didn't score your way?

A sound came from the woman's bag that was awfully familiar. Maybe the loud voices coming in from outside were playing with my brain. Again I heard it, distinctly sounding like a cat. A tiny paw reached out from under her hand. The woman was apparently shielding its eyes from the scene. "Oh, Princess Guinevere. It will be OK. Mommy will get you out of here soon and away from the bad man." The woman took another step away, almost to the door. "Please take care of this mess. I can't believe this is happening. Maybe I'll have to reconsider opening my bookstore here after all."

Uncle Jack looked at Cal and stepped between him and this lady. He tilted his head, bushy brows furrowed. "And who are you?"

The woman huffed, her hand still trying to cover the squirming cat. "Well, I'm Florence Kennedy, of course. Of the famous Kennedys."

Uncle Jack glanced at me and back at the woman. "Well, Flo, that doesn't answer my question."

The woman straightened up and stepped toward Uncle Jack. "That's Florence. And I bought this building. I came by to see it before I have everything moved in. I didn't know anyone would be here. Let alone a dead person." She flicked her arm around Uncle Jack toward Cal, then shivered like she was cold. Another meow from Florence's purse caused us all to look at her cat. "And Princess

Guinevere is so upset. I don't know if she will ever be the same again after seeing that." Again, she gestured toward Cal.

"Cats are resilient. She'll be fine. Why don't we go outside so we can talk?" A much louder meow came from the opposite side of the room. We all turned our heads and saw a black cat with white paws and a white chest strutting past Cal's body. "Oh, look. It's Willie," Uncle Jack said.

As Willie strolled past Cal, he took the opportunity to grab what must have been a piece of kite string and began playing with it. "Oh no," I said. "We should probably get him out of here so he doesn't mess with the crime scene." I took a step toward Willie and crouched. "Here, kitty, kitty."

Willie stopped batting the string for a moment and took a step in my direction. He quickly halted and resumed his play.

Uncle Jack said, "Let me try. He knows me. C'mon Willie. Let's get back home." He scooped Willie into his arm, getting a better look at Cal. "You're right, Tilly. That string looks like it may have been the murder weapon. It's wrapped around Cal's neck. I think it's kite string."

Florence gasped. "I had no idea this part of town was so rough. Why didn't the realtor tell me it was running rampant with hoodlums?" Princess Guinevere struggled to get her head out from under Florence's hand. Willie also began to seriously wiggle out of Uncle Jack's arms.

"We should probably get these two out of here before we end up like a scratching post. Florence, why don't you come next door to Checkered Past Antiques while we wait for the police?" Uncle Jack offered.

"Do you own that junk store?" she asked.

Uncle Jack's cheeks drooped and he frowned. That statement was a dagger to the heart. The store was his and his brother Frank's pride and joy. "I'll have you know, Flo, we have a lot of precious and high-end items. People travel from all over to come see us." Uncle Jack hugged Willie to his chest and stomped out of the building to the sidewalk.

I stepped to Uncle Jack's side and put my hand on his arm. "Is Willie your cat?"

He closed his eyes and shook his head. "No. He belongs to Justin who rents the apartment upstairs from the antique store." He tilted his head down the sidewalk toward Checkered Past Antiques. He turned to see if Florence was following him and entered his store. Uncle Jack put Willie on the floor and he took off like a rocket, taking shelter behind the display counter.

Florence stepped just barely inside and scanned the room, looking like she might reconsider Uncle Jack's offer.

"I'm going to call the police. You're welcome to take a seat while we wait," Uncle Jack said and gestured to a couple of chairs matching those on the outside of the store.

Looking down at her cat and pausing, Florence slowly made her way to the seat. She wiped her gloved hand across the fabric, removing any invisible dust and looking at her fingers. She made eye contact with Uncle Jack, shook her head, and sat on the edge of the chair. Princess Guinevere poked her head out of the bag with a huge sneeze. Florence gasped and put her hand over the cat's head again.

Willie peeked around the corner toward the sound he heard and looked at me. I shrugged. He looked at Princess Guinevere again and tiptoed a couple of steps toward her, wisely wary of the duo, who seemed completely out of place. I suspected after all of this drama, the deal for the purchase of the building next door would be null and void.

I didn't feel a need to engage Florence in conversation. This might be the last time we would see her. I heard Uncle Jack on the phone to the police, reporting our find. I was sure it wouldn't be long before someone would arrive to take our statements and gather clues from the scene. I hoped it would be soon. I was itching to get busy on my debut baking voyage. I could almost taste the cream that was part of Grandma Luna's legendary cupcakes. Thankfully, I now lived in a place that made it easier to get outside and be active. Tasting my treats would test my waistline. I sighed. I wanted more adventure in this new phase of my life. But finding dead bodies was not what I envisioned.

CHAPTER FOUR

"Good morning, Uncle Jack." I was so excited for my first day of baking I couldn't sleep the night before. "Where can I get some of that coffee?" I wove my way through the stacks of aisles teeming with merchandise. I held my breath, almost afraid of disturbing something and creating an avalanche.

"C'mon back. I've always got a pot going." He got a cup from the shelf and poured it full of the steaming elixir.

I took it, inhaled the aroma, and took a sip. I coughed. "Wow, that's strong stuff."

"I figured we would need it today. That was quite the first day you had yesterday." He took his coffee and sat in one of the chairs bordering the small table. He pointed at the other chair for me to sit. "Take a load off before we get too busy for our day."

I could learn a thing or two from my Uncle Jack about priorities and not stressing. He was as cool as a cucumber yesterday when that dead body appeared. Thankfully, due to his calm state I didn't freak out. At least on the outside. I was sure my restless night was also prompted by the mystery we had on our hands—and a murderer we had in our midst.

I sat and gripped the coffee cup with both hands, tipping and gulping half of it down. I felt an almost instant jolt from the caffeine. I looked at my uncle, slouched in his chair, gazing into the distance. He slowly turned and said, "I hope you don't let the events of yesterday scare you off. It really is safe here. Though, you probably had more of that to worry about in the big city."

I smiled. I didn't want to worry him. But I was scared. We certainly had a higher crime rate where I moved from, but never in my life had I seen a murdered body. "I'm OK. Your friend Barney was very gentle in his questioning yesterday. I think he even handled Florence well."

Barney Houston was the police chief of Belle Harbor. He probably dealt more with drunk and rowdy beach-goers than he did with dead bodies in this small town. But he acted like this was the millionth time he was investigating a murder.

I shivered at the thought of Cal laying on the floor, envisioning someone strangling him with kite string right next door. Did it happen when we were in the building? Or when we were on our walk? I racked my brain to remember anyone I happened to see near the antique store.

"Yeah, he's a pro. Barney and I go way back. He's been visiting more now that Frank has passed. He doesn't think I know what he's up to." Uncle Jack bowed his head, sat on the edge of his chair, and sighed. "Truth be told, I'm glad to see him. It has been lonely without my brother. I can't actually remember a time when Frank and I weren't together." His voice got quiet.

I scooted to the edge of my chair and got up to refill my cup. "I'm glad he's here for you."

Uncle Jack stood. "I do have a great friend group. That reminds me. We've got our weekly poker game Friday. Normally I'd close the store a bit early. But if you wouldn't mind?" He raised those bushy eyebrows toward me. How could I resist those—and this kind, gentle, supportive man?

"Of course I'll watch the shop for you, Unkie," I said.

He held out his hand to halt me pouring any more coffee. "Hold off on that a bit. I have a surprise for you." He put his empty cup on the table, grabbed my hand, and led me from the store. I was not one for surprises. I preferred having control of things in my life. For many years, I went along to get along. But that always felt like my life wasn't my own. I tried to organize and arrange what I could, but it was never enough. I was finally getting some clarity about my future that gave me peace. But with the Uncle Jack factor, I might just have to learn how to be more spontaneous.

We emerged onto the sidewalk along the beachfront shops. He guided me in the opposite direction than we had ventured yesterday. I couldn't fathom what he had in store for me. At this early hour, a few people were out and about. Mostly joggers on the boardwalk and a few families staking out their space on the beach for another day of the kite festival.

"Where are we going?" I looked over my shoulder at the antique shop. How in the world did he do so well in business when he frequently left the place unattended?

"Well, I figured you needed a better way to get around town to deliver your bakery items." He continued his brisk pace, causing me to start wheezing as I struggled to keep up.

"You're way ahead of me. I don't have any deliveries planned for a while. I was just going to sell the items from the antique shop," I said, gasping in between sentences.

Uncle Jack stopped. I suspected he realized he was running me ragged but didn't mention it. "Girl, you've got to be thinking big. You should go into Mocha Joe's and set up an arrangement with him to supply pastries. It would be a match made in heaven." He winked. Was he already setting me up for more than a business relationship? My stomach gurgled at the thought.

I slowed my pace and he matched my steps. "That's a good idea. I'll put it on my list to check out," I said. My breath finally steadied.

"Here we are," he said and turned into a Nelson's Moped Rental Shop. He grinned from ear to ear. "This will be perfect for you to get around town. We can get you one which has a basket to hold your deliveries."

"It's really too much. I can't," I said.

"Nonsense. I insist. Frank left money for me. And this is what I want to do. Hi Anna." Uncle Jack headed to the counter.

The woman waved. "Hi Jack. I'm all ready for you." Her long blonde hair bobbed behind her in a ponytail as she walked toward us. She pointed to the door of the shop.

"Beautiful Anna. This is my niece Tilly that I told you about."

Anna stuck her hand out and we shook. "Nice to meet you," I said and swung around and glared at Uncle Jack, my eyes wide.

"It's settled, I'm doing this for you." He led us outside to a row of three mopeds lined up against the front wall. Anna and I followed.

I stood with my hands on my hips, attempting to strike a pose of confidence. I had never ridden a moped. And my bicycle skills were quite rusty too. "I wouldn't know how to ride one."

Uncle Jack looked at Anna, and she handed him a key. "I'll show you. Easy peasy." He stepped up to the first moped in the row and swung his leg over it. He inserted the key and put on the helmet, pulling the strap snugly over his bushy beard. That man was bold.

I quickly stepped to his side and whispered, "Uncle Jack, what about your glaucoma?" I peeked at Anna. Did she not know that his eyesight wasn't the best? I had to stop this disaster waiting to happen.

"It's fine," he said.

I didn't know how it could be fine. "Why doesn't Anna show me?" I looked at her for support in my pleas.

"Tilly." He called me over and tipped his head in a conspiratorial manner, looking over my shoulder at Anna. He said, "Justin hooked me up with some marijuana. It's really helped." He sat tall. "Just watch." I hoped I wasn't about to see the end of my uncle. He started the moped and sped off down the sidewalk, out to the boardwalk.

My heart raced and I shook my head. Anna stepped up next to me. "He thinks his glaucoma 'treatment,'"—she used air quotes—"is illegal. We keep telling him that it's legal now to have marijuana. But I think he likes believing he's doing something nefarious. It really does seem to help his eyesight."

I took a deep breath and watched my uncle speed along the boardwalk, earning him a few dirty looks from the early morning beach crowd. At that moment, I had no doubt the universe had put him and I together at this point in time—just what we both needed in our lives.

I talked Uncle Jack into riding the moped back to the antique store until I could get more practice driving it. That might have been against my better judgment as he whizzed past me and several people, one hand waving in the air, yelling 'yeehaw.' I closed my eyes and gulped, saying a silent prayer that he would return in one piece. It was no wonder he was a free spirit as the son of Grandma Luna, who always danced to her own music. The sun had now risen, beginning to warm up the growing crowd on the beach.

The colorful Ferris wheel was now running with a long line of people waiting for their ride. The rhythmic sound of the waves coming to shore slowed my heartrate. I inhaled the salt air. The ambiance in Belle Harbor was something I could easily get used to. A feeling of freedom, a permanent vacation, and a whole new life lay before me.

My goal was to focus on becoming the best baker I could. The temporary spot Uncle Jack had created in the Checkered Past Antiques' store would do until I established my business. I looked ahead and saw Unkie had parked the moped and returned to the store. I couldn't wait to see what life had in store for me. It had to be better than up 'til now. This was going to be a great day.

CHAPTER FIVE

No doubt the sea air and the excitement of the last couple of days exhausted me for a good night's sleep. The sun was up, and I felt like I was already behind for my day. Bakers started their shifts by 4:00 a.m., and it was several hours after that. I just couldn't bring myself to ride my new moped yet, so I walked the few blocks from my little rental cottage to the antique store. I rounded the corner to the sidewalk along the beachfront shops and saw the Checkered Past Antiques' door propped open and ready for business. Light blazed through the front window, illuminating the bench in front of the store.

I entered the shop and didn't see a soul. Two deep voices came from the table and chairs in the corner that Uncle Jack had set up for his coffee chats. I teased him that it was his good ole boys club.

"Over here, Tilly," came Uncle Jack's voice as I saw fingers wiggling in the air. The smell of coffee started my taste buds salivating. I needed a jolt of java to get my day going.

"Hi guys," I said, reaching for the cup of coffee Uncle Jack handed me. "You're here early."

Uncle Jack pointed to a chair for me to be seated and join their little group. He looked over at Barney, back at me, and returned to his chair. "Yeah, I guess I don't like rattling around in that big house by myself." He looked off in the distance, peering over the stacks of antiques filling the room.

I looked at Barney and raised my eyebrows. It was relatively recent since Uncle Frank had passed. Those two brothers had been inseparable from day one. It must have felt like a part of your body had been removed when your lifelong companion was suddenly gone. I reached over and grabbed Unkie's hand. He looked at me and tilted his head, smiling with pursed lips. "You look so much like her. It's almost as if she is actually here." From as early as I could remember, everyone told me that I was the spitting image of Grandma Luna. At first, I bristled at those comments. Who wanted to be compared to an old woman when you were a young girl? Now I took it as the highest compliment.

"I only hope I can do the bakery justice," I said.

"Tilly, I have a question," Barney interjected. I bet all of Uncle Jack's friends had lots of questions about his niece suddenly showing up on the scene. They were a protective group, and I was sure they were skeptical about a relative coming to take over his business.

"Yes?" I said, drawing out the word into multiple syllables.

"It's really none of my business," Barney started. He stood and grabbed the coffee carafe to refill his cup. He returned to his seat, stirring the coffee with a spoon clinking the sides of the cup. Keeping his focus on the coffee, he continued, "Why don't you stay with Jack? He's got lots of room in that house."

Thankfully, Uncle Jack and I had already discussed this topic. And it was settled, at least for now. I boldly sat up in my chair and said,

"I've never really lived by myself. I've wanted to have that experience for a while."

Barney looked at Uncle Jack and shrugged as if silently messaging *I tried.*

I finished my coffee and set my empty cup on the table. "I better get to it. Those cupcakes aren't going to make themselves." I rubbed my hands together. "Uncle Jack, it looks like you've been busy rearranging again." I walked along a couple of tables and noticed several items had been moved. "Maybe my organization system is rubbing off on you." I laughed. That would never happen.

He stood and looked over the many tables displaying everything from 1800's telephones to 1700's typewriters. "No. Why do you say that?"

I turned to see if he was joking. He rubbed his chin. He took several steps between the tables, examining the items. He looked back at me. "Nope, maybe a customer did that." He picked up a couple of items and moved them to a different location. "There," he said and returned to his chair next to Barney, seeming to be satisfied he had righted everything.

"Barney, what's the latest on Cal's death?" Uncle Jack was back to the coffee corner. "That woman we met over there was pretty upset. I think she felt put out because someone had dared die in her building."

"Yeah, I don't think she would take too kindly to you referring to her as *that woman*." Barney chuckled.

My baker workspace was close enough to the coffee corner that I could still participate in the conversation, or at least eavesdrop. I began gathering all of my ingredients and tools in preparation for making the cupcakes. I had two willing taste-testers at my beck and call. Even though they were friendlies, I was still nervous about sharing my work.

"Well, you saw the kite string," Barney continued. "What I've learned is that it's a type that is expensive and that very few people use for kite flying. It's mostly found in competitions. That might narrow down the list of suspects to someone likely to have that."

"Uncle Jack?" I put my hands on my hips and looked around my little mini bakery. I could have sworn some of the supplies I had were previously in different locations.

"Yes, dear?" He stood and peered over a pile of antiques.

"Did you happen to move some of the bakery supplies?" I shook my head. As I looked around the storage, almost everything had been put in another location. I opened drawers and cabinets to locate what I was going to need for the cupcakes. It might take me a half hour just to find everything.

"Well, of course. I wanted to make it easier for you to find what you needed," he said.

Bless his heart for trying. But we would have to discuss some boundaries. He could keep to his antiques and I would keep to my bakery. I braced myself for another scavenger hunt, and I looked for the cupcake pan and paper liners. I knew I had everything, somewhere.

The quiet of the room was suddenly shattered with the sound of an old-fashioned phone ringing. I jumped, spilling my cup of flour down the front of my apron. Well, at least now I officially looked like a baker. I wasn't surprised that Uncle Jack hadn't upgraded his business phone to the twenty-first century. The phone rang a second time, and I lifted my head to see if he was going to answer it.

"Jack, I think that old phone over there is the one that's ringing." Barney stood and gazed at the direction of the sound. The phone rang again. He looked back at Uncle Jack. "Yep. Now I'm sure of it." His eyes widened.

"Oh, it does that every now and then. Ever since I plugged it in about two or three times a week it will randomly go off," Uncle Jack said.

I left my bakery and approached the phone. It rang again. I wiped my hands on my apron and answered it. "Hello?" I looked around at Jack and Barney. "Hello?" I repeated.

Uncle Jack reached my side. "There's never anyone there when it rings. I try to answer when I can." He took the receiver from my hand and hung it up, then picked it up again. "There's no dial tone, so I'm not sure why it rings."

I headed back to continue my baking. "That's kind of creepy."

"That's what the older gentleman said when he brought it in. His wife was tired of it ringing all the time, so he wanted to get rid of it." He picked up the receiver again and held it to his ear for a few seconds, then replaced it on the hook. "I kind of like the character it has. I like to think maybe it's someone from beyond trying to get in touch, and they just keep trying until the right person answers."

Perhaps he was hoping it might be his brother one of these times. My heart ached for his loss. Uncle Frank was in a lot of ways just like Uncle Jack. They both loved life. I missed him too.

"Well, Jack, I need to head back to the office. I'll keep you posted on any developments in Cal's case." Uncle Jack escorted Barney to the door. It gave me the shivers not knowing what happened right next door. I hoped they would soon have answers. I turned my focus to my cupcakes. Having this first batch turn out well would take all of my concentration. And if they did, I planned to take them to Florence as a peace offering. We didn't start off well. And if we were going to be business neighbors, it would be good for everyone if we got along.

CHAPTER SIX

While my cupcakes were cooling, I decided to take a stroll outside. The leader board of the kite competition read the same as before, looking like Burkhart might in fact pull off an upset. With Cal out of the picture they had a replacement judge sitting at the table. Truth be told, I was trying to work off some nervous energy for my first baking attempt in my new space. Even though I hadn't finished culinary school, I had acquired all of the basics. Due to my move from Boston, completing my studies had to be put on hold.

But Uncle Jack made me promise that when I arrived I would let him pay for me to finish school. I agreed but secretly hoped I was so good he wouldn't have to use his money.

My lungs filled with fresh air, I returned to my kitchen to finish the cupcakes. Using the pastry bag full of cream, I loaded each cupcake with the sweet vanilla. This was one area where I planned to experiment with different flavors. I wanted to have a variety to supply customer's requests of cupcakes, frostings, and fillings. The next batch of cupcakes up was almond batter and coconut filling. Why not go tropical since we were at the beach?

I finished filling each one and stood back to admire my handiwork. A few cupcakes had bigger holes than others, but those would just get more frosting to cover the blemishes. And who didn't want more frosting? I topped off each cupcake with the chocolate glaze. I chose the best-looking one, sprinkled a little powdered sugar on for garnish, plated it, and went in search for Uncle Jack. Thankfully, with me in the antiques store now, his absence wasn't as much of a concern that an unattended business would get ripped off.

As Uncle Jack returned from the beach, I met him at the door, sweat beads dotting his bald head. "Whew, it's a warm one today. And I don't just mean the weather. I really think that Burkhart is going to pull off an upset," he said. He looked at my outstretched hands and grinned widely. "Is this what I think it is?"

I matched his smile and nodded. "I want you to have the first one."

He put his hand on his heart. "You should join me. And we should toast this momentous occasion." He led me back to the coffee corner. I wouldn't have been surprised if he had pulled out a bottle of hooch, even at this early hour. I was quickly learning to expect the unexpected from Uncle Jack. He poured us each a cup of coffee. We clinked cups and said "cheers." Uncle Jack inserted about half of the cupcake in his mouth. Immediately his eyes widened, and not in a *this is the best thing I've tasted* expression, but instead in more of a *this thing is hideous* kind of look.

"What's wrong with it?" I asked and scooted to the edge of my chair, looking at the half-eaten cupcake on his plate. At first glance, it looked fine. How could I have messed it up? My face flushed and tears blurred my vision.

He shook his head and held out his hand in a halting gesture, swallowing in a large gulp. He swallowed again as if to rid his mouth of the horrible taste. "No, I think for your first one, it's OK."

It didn't seem OK. And if my biggest fan didn't like it, I wouldn't have any customers. "I don't understand. I followed the recipe to a T," I said. I stood and picked up his plate with the remaining cupcake. I examined it from all sides. It looked moist and delicious. I tossed the cupcake in the trash and the plate with it. I held my head in my hands.

Unkie came up from behind me and put his arm around my shoulders. He quietly said, "I'm sure even professional bakers throw out a lot of their first tries. You'll get it." He wiped a tear from my cheek.

"But if I can't even follow a simple recipe like an amateur, how will I ever be a professional?" I wiped my tears on my sleeve and stomped back to the baking area, slamming things around for the cleanup.

Uncle Jack followed me. "Tilly, give yourself a break, OK?" He stepped around the counter and said, "Here, let me help you."

We silently cleaned the mess. All the while I pouted that I wasn't perfect. So what if I had to keep working at it? Was he right? Maybe if I returned to school and kept at it, I might get better. I had to place all my hopes on that. My dream of Luna's Bakery had to stay alive. Because otherwise... I couldn't let my mind go there. The dishes sat in the dishwasher, and we finished storing the ingredients for next time. I picked up the pastry bag of cream and looked a little closer at it. Normally, with the vanilla flavoring it would be a slight off-white color. But the filling was a bright, stark white. Could that be my mistake? I squeezed a dollop onto my finger and tasted it. Yep, pure shortening. How could I have made that big of a mistake?

"This is it. I held out the bag. Somehow there's shortening in this bag instead of the cream filling I made." I perked up a bit. If I found the cause of the problem, I could fix it. Silly me. I hadn't even tasted one of my own cupcakes. I took a big bite of the chocolate to get some of the filling. My eyes bulged. Gross. I spit the cupcake out and gave Uncle Jack a huge hug. "Maybe I can do this after all." I clapped my hands and took a stuttering breath. OK. That was a good test for how I handled setbacks. An area for improvement, for sure. "Oh, I'm so relieved to figure it out."

Uncle Jack approached me and held both of my hands, locking eyes. "Um, Tilly. I have a confession."

My cheeks sagged. What was all of a sudden so serious? "What is it Uncle Jack?" I took a step closer to him, looking deep into his eyes. My mind could go from zero to catastrophe in about two seconds. I hoped this wasn't some bad news about his health. From everything I had seen, the man was as healthy as a horse. His endurance could certainly outdo me.

"I was only trying to help," he said.

"I don't understand," I replied.

He stepped around me and picked up the pastry bag with the shortening inside, holding it out for me to see. "I thought these bags were for shortening. So I filled them up from the cans to make it easier for you to measure. I guess it got mixed up with the cream filling you made." His voice wavered.

I jumped up and pounced on him with a bear hug, then laughed and held his hand. "Tell you what. Why don't we make a deal? You are totally in charge of the antiques. And I'm totally in charge of the bakery. If the other one would like help, we can offer our services?"

"You're not mad?" he asked.

"I will never be mad at you, ever. Uncle Jack, you have always had the biggest heart for others. From the time I was old enough to come visit you and Uncle Frank, your generosity and kindness were overwhelming."

"I like your suggestion," he said. He grabbed the tray of cupcakes and slid them into the garbage can. "Just like they never existed. I promise I'll stay out of your way from now on."

"If your stomach can handle it, I would still like you to be my taste-tester. But I won't ask you to try anything I haven't first tried myself."

"Deal," he said, and we shook on it.

A loud bang came from the other side of the wall that we shared with Florence's Bookstore. We both looked at each other. "I didn't think anyone would be in there yet. I wonder what's going on?" I asked.

Uncle Jack took off like a rocket. "One way to find out."

I scurried to keep up with him and put some distance between me and that shortening filling. I shuddered, reliving that terrible taste. Never again.

CHAPTER SEVEN

———ele———

The door to the bookstore was propped open, just like at the antique shop. I was sure it could use some thorough airing out from being vacant. But, you know, from the dead body too. I only hoped we wouldn't find another mysterious situation on our hands. I followed Uncle Jack inside to scout out the source of the noise. He abruptly stopped, and I bumped him from behind, uttering, "Umph."

Furniture filled the entire room, scattered every which way. Bookshelves, tables, chairs. Boxes upon boxes of books. And in the far corner, already completely set up was a fully furnished tearoom. A small round table was adorned with a flowing tablecloth designed with pink roses. Light pink chairs surrounded the table, which had four place settings of saucers, cups, and cloth napkins. Behind the table in the corner was a gold lamp with a beige lampshade and large pink bow. And towering above it all was an oval mirror that must have been six feet in diameter.

Uncle Jack stepped through the door and panned the room. "Ah, Flo. I mean Florence. There you are." He moved further into the fray, weaving between the piles. "We heard a bang and wanted to see if everything was OK."

Florence wore a different dress from the other day, flowered with pink roses that matched the tablecloth and with two sets of pearls around her neck—and her sensible heels. As sensible as heels could be. Still tucked into her purse was Princess Guinevere. I wondered if she wouldn't mind me calling her cat PG for short. That name was a mouthful. Though I was sure that reference would offend her based on the vibe I got.

She came toward us, stroking her cat. "No. Put that against the wall," she ordered the movers and pointed. She stopped in front of Uncle Jack, her feet planted wide, appearing ready for battle. She looked him up and down. And I would swear she sniffed.

Whether he was aware of the slight, I couldn't tell. But my kind uncle said, "You're making great progress. You'll be open in no time." He looked around. There was a ton of work to do. But judging by the number of people helping, he was probably right.

"No thanks to the neighborhood. That person's body in here almost made me cancel my purchase contract." Princess Guinevere quietly meowed from the bag attached to Florence's shoulder. "But I wouldn't be deterred. This bookstore is my destiny."

Uncle Jack snickered, and his mouth slightly tilted up in a grin. "Are you serving tea?"

Florence turned her head. "Oh, not to you." She halted, possibly realizing how rude her comment was. Or not. "I mean, we will have tea for our book clubs."

I was pretty sure Uncle Jack would have no interest in her book clubs or tea. That just didn't seem like his thing. He said, "We want to wish you the best of luck for your store." He stretched his arm toward her to shake hands.

She looked at his hand and instead returned to petting her cat. "I just hope my Gwinnie recovers from the trauma. She has never seen"—she put her hand up to her mouth, turned away from her cat, and whispered—"a dead body before."

Uncle Jack looked at me, eyes wide, as if to say *this woman's a bit of a loon*. I gave a slight nod.

Gwinnie looked up at Florence, let out a loud yowl, and leapt from the purse. Florence squealed and with both arms reaching tried to capture the escaping cat. The aisles were too small for Florence to make much progress. "She's probably just stressed from all of the drama." Florence looked back at us and touched her hair to straighten the imaginary stray strand. "I need to get back to work. Lots to do," she said and lifted her arm. It appeared her work was ordering the movers around.

She stopped in her tracks, and right in front of her, Gwinnie and another cat were circling each other. Florence looked back at us and pointed at Willie who had invaded her space. Florence's voice raised a couple of octaves she said, "Get your cat out of here! Why do people think they can just come and go in this place?" She took two steps toward the cats, who were now nuzzling each other. "Stop that, you mangy cat. Leave my Gwinnie alone." She reached toward Gwinnie to scoop her up, and the cat stepped just out of reach. "Oh, this is turning into the worst day ever."

The cats moved further back into the stacks of boxes. "Dang, Willie. How did you get in here?" We all turned in unison to the voice coming from the doorway. If the man was referring to Willie, this must be his owner, Justin.

I took a step back and put my hand on my heart. Uncle Jack mentioned the guy renting the apartment above the antique store, but he failed to tell me how good looking he was. Justin had the surfer-guy thing going on. Mussed up, wavy blond hair. Muscles protruding from his snug, short-sleeved faded T-shirt. Shorts and flip-flops. The whole package. The muscles in my diaphragm tightened, restricting my breath. *Simmer down, Tilly.* I took a slow, deep breath and forced my gaze away from Justin.

Florence stormed toward Justin and poked her finger in his direction. "You need to keep your alley cat away from my princess. And out of my store, everyone. We have a lot of work to do." She turned and approached one of the workers, pointing at several pieces of furniture.

Justin moved further into the store, saying, "Geez. She could use some calming beach vibes." He winked at Uncle Jack, as if that was some kind of code. "Hey, Willie." He reached the cats and scooped them both into his arms. "What's this?"

Everyone turned to see what Justin referred to. He held up part of a kite tail that both Willie and Gwinnie had in their mouth, like the spaghetti noodle and the two dogs in *Lady and the Tramp*. The orange ribbon dangled in his hand.

Uncle Jack stepped toward Justin and took the ribbon. Examining all sides, he looked up and said, "That's part of the tail of Maverick's kite."

Florence gasped and her hand flew to her mouth. "Will it ever end?" She whimpered, shaking her head. She grabbed Gwinnie from Justin's arm and stuffed the cat into her bag.

Justin stroked Willie's back. I could hear the purring from where I stood. Willie had a new girlfriend. *Let the games begin.* "The other thing," Justin started, clamping his mouth closed.

Florence's head flew up. "What now?" she yelled.

Justin pointed behind some boxes. In the dust in the corner, it looked like there were some footprints.

Florence pounded her heels in the direction Justin indicated. He touched her arm. "Don't go there."

She glared at him. "This is my store, and I'll go where I want to. Those cleaners obviously did a poor job and they won't get a dime from me."

"Well, maybe that's a good thing," Justin said.

Florence squinted at him.

"What I mean is that one set of the footprints looks like it's a pair of specialty shoes that you wear for gripping sand. Sometimes volleyball players have them. But I've recently seen kite fliers wearing them too so they have some resistance in controlling those large kites." Justin looked around the room as we all stared, like he was giving a performance.

Uncle Jack moved to the center of the group. "I think we all need to get out of here for the time being to let the police return and continue the investigation into Cal's death." He panned the circle, and we were all bobbing our heads.

Florence sniffled and Uncle Jack went to escort her out. "Don't worry. I'll come help you finish moving in after the police give the all clear," he said. That man could sweet talk and encourage the crustiest of personalities. Good thing, since she would be our business neighbor; they would no doubt have a lot of time with each other.

I took a deep breath. Maybe the clues were piling up in favor of one of the kite-flying competitors. It sure looked like an open-and-shut case. I only hoped it would be resolved soon. I didn't have any fear for my safety. But the pallor cast over the town by this mysterious death would not be good for tourism. The workers exited the store, and we followed Uncle Jack and Florence, quietly closing the door behind us.

CHAPTER EIGHT

ell

The sleep of the dead was now a distant memory for me. No amount of exhaustion from the work or sea air to clear my lungs and mind could have provided me any rest last night. I knew adjusting to a new place would take some time. Everything in my little bungalow cottage was new. It was sparsely decorated until I could afford a few more items, but I was insistent that I wanted nothing from my old life. I craved a fresh start. Despite spending money on a quality bed, it had not quite lived up to the advertisement proving better sleep. Perhaps in time.

And the fact that my neighbor kept a few egg-laying chickens in his yard did not help. Thankfully, there was no crowing rooster. But early in the morning I could hear those little ladies taking care of business. Clucking and clawing for food and laying their eggs.

I looked forward to another day of baking, my happy place. The antique shop was only a few blocks from my cottage. I could easily walk the distance but decided it would be the perfect distance to practice a small amount of moped riding. Helmet strapped on and backpack in place, I slowly goosed the accelerator. Before I knew it, I had peeled rubber and was speeding toward the beach. One turn of the handle propelled me almost halfway to the store. I removed my hand from the accelerator to let the machine coast the remainder of the way. My heart raced. Thankfully, no one was harmed in my trial run.

The machine sputtered the last few feet to the front of the store and died. I looked down, hoping to see something obvious causing this, but I knew nothing about motor vehicles. I stepped off the moped and pushed it to a spot out of the way. Great. I broke it already. Or maybe there was some secret button I needed to know about.

"Hey, your inaugural ride. Great job!" Always the encourager, Uncle Jack. He stood in the doorway to the store.

"Except I think I broke it. It died just as I got it here." I removed my helmet and slipped out of my backpack.

Uncle Jack took my helmet and we headed back to the coffee corner. "Let's go see Anna in a bit. Maybe she has some history on that thing that could help. Hopefully, we didn't get you a lemon right off the bat."

I set my backpack on the floor and pulled out a notebook and pen. Unkie handed me some coffee. I inhaled and closed my eyes. "I'm probably going to need several of these to get going today."

"You didn't sleep well?" He sat in the chair on the opposite side of the table.

"Nah, lots going on. And my neighbor's chickens are early birds." I took a gulp of the coffee. Already my brain was waking up.

He reached his arm across the table and tipped his head. "Tilly, give it time. You've had a lot of change in a small amount of time."

I sighed and my shoulders slumped. "I know. But I have big goals. And I'm impatient." I smiled at him.

"All in due time, girl. Don't be so hasty to wish your life away. Enjoy the journey as well," he said. I put my cup on the table and gave him a hug. "And I'm sorry for all of the nonsense next door. That can't be helping your transition."

I sat and took another drink of coffee, finishing the cup. "Well, I'm going to my happy place. Planning the next things I'm going to make. I got to thinking about your suggestion to get my name out there. Later when we come back from the moped shop, let's stop in at Mocha Joe's. I have some ideas to propose." Just thinking about that conversation made my hands sweat. I wiped them on my pants.

"Yes!" he yelled. "I knew you'd eventually come around. I just wish you could see yourself the same as others see you. An extremely capable woman."

"OK. Enough of the mutual admiration society for now." I tapped my pen on my notebook. "I'm thinking I will offer some bran flax muffins." I had found a great healthy recipe that I assumed would be well received. I would source local and organic ingredients as much as possible, which would also allow me to charge higher prices.

"What happened to your sweet treats?" He looked at me, his expression slack, a whiny tone to his voice.

"Uncle Jack, I don't want to send everyone into a sugar high all the time. I'll have those too. But I'd like to offer choices."

"Well, as long as you don't force me to eat those poop producers all the time, I guess I can get on board with that."

I clipped my pen to my notebook and headed to the kitchen. "Deal. But I want you around for a long time." I planned another go at the cream-filled cupcakes, sans my helper filling my pastry bag with shortening this time. Just knowing what happened the first round boosted my confidence. I planned to bake a batch as a peace offering for Florence. I could have Uncle Jack bring them to her to help mend that relationship.

"Can I help you find something?" I heard Uncle Jack say. I raised on my tiptoes to see who had entered the store. I might suggest he add some kind of a doorbell that goes off when someone comes in. Especially if I was alone in the store all the way in the kitchen corner.

"Maybe," the woman said and continued to look along the tables. The intensity of her search appeared as if she was looking for something specific. Uncle Jack followed her from place to place. She stopped and looked at him as if just noticing his presence. She pushed her glasses up and said, "I'm looking for a pocket watch. A very specific pocket watch." She sidestepped Uncle Jack and continued scouring the tables.

Despite the apparent disorganization, Uncle Jack seemed to have a surprisingly good handle on what he had and where it was at. "If you can describe it a bit more, I can tell you if I have it."

The woman turned toward him and pursed her bright red lips. "I don't know how you could have a clue what's in this mess," she said in a condescending tone. She picked up a small birdcage and removed it from the top of a silver goblet.

Uncle Jack stepped forward and took the birdcage from her hand, returning it to its spot. "I'm here to help. Seriously, if you can give me a description, I promise I can tell you if we have it."

She reached into her purse and pulled out a piece of paper, unfolded it, and handed it to Uncle Jack. She pointed to the picture on the paper and said, "I'm looking for the Imperial officer's pocket watch. It's one of the most expensive ever made. Just like that." She tapped the paper for emphasis.

Uncle Jack looked up from the paper and said, "Well, I can tell you we don't have that. But I do have some very nice pocket watches." He turned and started around the other side of the table.

"No," she said. "It has to be that one. And I don't want to buy it."

I was more confused than ever watching this exchange.

Uncle Jack stopped and tilted his head, his bushy eyebrows furrowed.

"What I mean is," the woman started. She followed Uncle Jack and retrieved the piece of paper from him, folded it, and returned it to her purse. She shook her head. "Someone stole this from me, and I'm going around to antique shops to see if anyone sold it."

"I'm so sorry," he gently replied. "If you can give me your name and number, I will be sure to let you know if I see it."

"I'll be back if I don't find it." She turned and left the store.

I left the kitchen and followed the woman's path out the door, looking both ways as I got to the sidewalk. I returned and said, "That was bizarre."

Uncle Jack shrugged. "Maybe. You might be surprised at some of the kooky customers I get in this antique store. Each piece," he said, lifting the birdcage again and twirling it, "has a story." He set it down in the same location the woman had placed it, apparently deciding maybe she had a point with her comment about the clutter.

I wiped my hands on my apron. "Tell you what. After I get this batch of cupcakes out of the oven, let's head to the moped store."

"Mmhmm," he replied, distracted. He picked up a couple things, a typewriter, a stagecoach with accompanying horses and rider, and a brass tea kettle. He arranged them more along the lines of how I would display them, in neat orderly rows. I really hoped he wasn't second-guessing himself because of that woman.

CHAPTER NINE

Thankfully, the delicious aroma of my desserts didn't add to my waistline. I pulled the chocolate cupcakes from the oven and placed them on a cooling rack. I untied my apron and hung it on hook shaped like a little spatula.

"All right, Uncle Jack. I'm ready to head to the moped store." I scanned the room and found him continuing to rearrange like a madman. I had to admit, it did make it easier for people to see what was there. "Looks good," I said.

He harrumphed. I didn't think he wanted to admit that woman had a point, especially given her rudeness. My uncle was kind and forgiving. And I think she hurt his feelings.

I touched his elbow. "This is your business. You get to run it the way you want." I pulled the moped keys out of my backpack. Might as well see if the thing would start, even for just the short trip.

"I don't want anyone ever to say this old dog can't learn a new trick or two." He set the model ship down that he had been holding. He reached over and adjusted its angle. "I've just been reluctant to change much after Frank passed." He further arranged the ship's placement.

"I'm sorry." I put my arm around his shoulders. "I'm sure he would be fine with what you want to do." I looked at him and brushed the escaping tear from his cheek.

"Yeah, he would probably be kicking my butt for waiting so long." He chuckled. "That man didn't mince words." He sniffled. "That's why we made such a good team."

We turned and headed out the door. My initial reluctance at leaving the store unattended waned just the slightest. But I didn't know if I would ever get used to that. I swung my leg over the moped and inserted the key. Uncle Jack looked at me and held up crossed fingers. I turned the key and the engine moaned. I turned it off. It was worth a try.

Uncle Jack took the moped by the handlebars and pushed it as we began our short trek. Even though the kite festival was over, the throngs were just as big. I guess any excuse would get people to the beach. Every time I exited the antique store onto the sidewalk, the soothing sound of the waves hit me. I could easily see how Uncle Jack and Uncle Frank had made this their home for so many decades.

"I'm so glad I moved here," I said and looked at Unkie. He wasn't even breaking a sweat pushing that thing. Though, the mid-eighty degree day was still several hours away and we would be dripping in no time.

"You ain't seen nothin' yet," he replied.

"Should I be worried?" I laughed.

"There's so much here that I want to share with you." He grinned. "That salt-water taffy store." He flicked his head up and to the right. "Daffy Taffy. They have almost a hundred flavors. Just when I've tried them all, they make more."

"You really do have a sweet tooth, Uncle Jack." The taffy store was painted with large pink and white vertical stripes on the side walls.

The topmost part of the wall had a horizontal pink stripe with taffy in white wrappers. The door was a light teal, also with taffy in multiple-colored wrappers. They had a large front window where you could watch them pulling the sticky, sweet candy.

"They also have tasting nights when they're trying out a bunch of new flavors. You could do that too. Have a tasting with different kinds of pastry."

I hastened my walk as Uncle Jack was hitting his stride, my breath still catching as I tried to keep up. "I like that idea," I said.

"But," he said and looked at me in all seriousness, "don't do like me and lose your dentures during the tasting. That's not a good look."

I paused, waiting for his punch line. He continued his brisk pace. "OK, so noted," I said and tipped my chin down, hoping he couldn't hear my snickering.

I took a deep breath, trying to generate a second wind before we arrived and I wasn't able to speak at all.

Uncle Jack slowed down and leaned the moped against the railing in front of Nelson's Moped Rental Shop. I followed him inside as we searched for the worker. There wasn't a soul in sight. People here really did have an openness and trust I had never seen before. He put his hand up to the side of his mouth. "Hello, hello, hello," he said in the form of an echo. He looked at me and smiled, finding small joys in every experience.

"Oh, hi there," a male voice said from behind us. "Do you want to rent some mopeds?"

We wheeled around. The nametag on the young man said Cooper. Uncle Jack leaned forward like he was studying the name and raised his head, looking the young man in the eye. "Where's Anna?" He looked around like he expected her to jump out and yell *surprise*.

"Oh," Cooper said quietly, moving behind the counter and fiddling around straightening some papers. "She doesn't work here anymore."

Uncle Jack took a step closer. "Is she OK?" He stretched out his arm, as if to comfort Cooper.

Cooper shrugged. "Yeah. Um, did you want to rent?" He looked at me for clarification.

I stepped forward. "No. We bought a moped the other day, and it's having issues running. I'm hoping you have a mechanic that can take a look at it."

"Sure. I'll have to check Alan's schedule and let you know. Do you have it here with you?"

"Why doesn't Anna work here anymore?" Uncle Jack continued. I wondered where his mind was that he was so concerned about her welfare.

"I really shouldn't be talking about this," Cooper said, fidgeting with his ear. He looked around and leaned in. He mouthed, *she got fired.*

"What? Why?" Uncle Jack demanded answers.

"I'm really going to get in trouble for talking about this." Cooper looked around again. "Can you show me where the moped is and give me the keys?" His look implored me to stop the grilling from Uncle Jack. He took the keys and I led us to the sidewalk.

"I'll take full responsibility," Uncle Jack said.

Cooper inhaled and huffed. His jaw muscles flexed. He must have concluded that the only way out of this was through it. Once last covert glance around and he blurted, "She was badmouthing the owner and his business. I guess she just did it one too many times."

"Does it run at all?" Cooper asked me.

"It sounds like it will start but then doesn't," I said. Explaining car things was way outside my knowledge and expertise.

"Let me talk to the manager or Nelson. I know I can get her job back," Uncle Jack pleaded.

Cooper had both handlebars of the moped and began pushing it around the corner to the back of the building.

"Nelson is just the business name. It's actually owned by Cal Borman." Cooper let go of one of the handlebars and gripped his left hand around his neck. He turned and disappeared with the ailing moped.

"That poor girl," Uncle Jack said. He plopped onto the bench with his head in his hands. "She needed that job. I have to see if there's something I can do to help."

"I know you mean well. But I don't know if getting a disgruntled employee rehired is the best choice. Maybe it was a blessing in disguise for her to move on to another place."

He shook his head, running his fingers through his thinning hair. I put my hand on his back and lightly patted.

"Maybe. I'll think about it." His body slumped. Dejected, he said, "We should probably get back." And we were off.

CHAPTER TEN

Without a word, we proceeded on our return route to Checkered Past Antiques. I figured we would stop by the coffee shop another day. That gave me relief and would mean I could do some more experimenting before making a business deal.

On a dime, Uncle Jack pivoted ninety degrees to the left and entered Mocha Joe's Coffee Shop. I stood outside, stunned. I put my hands on my hips and waited. When he realized I hadn't followed him inside, he came back to the door.

The neon outline of a steaming cup of coffee blinked in the front window.

"No time like the present," he said, grinning. He bounced on his feet, waiting for me to budge. My stomach was in my throat. Maybe it was the best time. No chance to get any more nervous than I already was and try to back out at the last second. I gulped and stepped inside. There wasn't a smell much better than fresh ground coffee beans and fresh brewed coffee. I followed Uncle Jack to the counter.

A man about forty years old was behind the counter serving a customer. He wore a light blue button-down shirt with sleeves rolled up to his elbows. Over the top was a bright orange apron that said *Mocha Joe's Coffee Shop*.

Uncle Jack and I waited our turn, and when the man saw us, he burst into a giant smile. "Hi Jack," he said and then turned to me and said, "You must be Tilly."

I nodded, unable to utter a word to this gorgeous guy. Uncle Jack looked at me and put a hand on my shoulder. "Tilly has a business proposition to talk to you about." He continued to look at me.

After an awkward amount of silence, I cleared my throat, "Um, yeah. I have a business proposition for you, Mocha Joe."

He chuckled. "You can just call me Joe. I'm excited to hear it. When Jack mentioned you were moving to town and opening a bakery, my wheels started churning. I think you've got a lot of potential for multiple avenues of business around town." He removed his apron and came around the counter. He grabbed a notebook and pen and pointed to a table along the wall. "Why don't we sit for a minute to chat. Callie can take over for me for now." The teenage girl looked at us and grinned to show a mouth full of braces.

We followed Joe to the table and sat. I tried to inconspicuously inhale deeply to calm my nerves. I couldn't tell if they were frayed due to the business discussion or the fact it was being held with a good-looking man. I was in no way interested in dating for quite some time, if ever.

Joe sat across from me and Uncle Jack sat to my side. "I just want to say, I hope you don't judge our quaint little town by the recent events," Joe said. "Any updates, Jack?"

Uncle Jack shook his head. "Not much. There's been a few clues found. It's pointing to someone involved in kite flying from what I can see. But Barney is keeping the good stuff close to his vest for now."

"I'm sure we'll know soon. On to happier stuff." Joe smiled at me. "Why don't you go first, Tilly? I'd love to have your input before I bombard you with my hairbrained schemes."

"Joe, you're too modest. You've got excellent business sense, from what I can tell," Uncle Jack interjected. He looked at me. My turn. *OK brain, please click in so I don't look like a total fool.*

I scooted my chair forward and put my hands in my lap. "I haven't gotten everything worked out yet." Joe sat forward with his elbows on the table, the notebook and pen pushed aside. "But I've got a few ideas. I'd like to offer options for pastries that are locally sourced and organic, along with the classic items. But I'm very open to what you think would sell." There. I didn't totally flub it, I hoped.

"Great," Joe said. "That's just about what I was thinking."

"I knew you two would be a great match," Uncle Jack said. Joe and I swiveled our heads toward him. "In business, I meant." He held up a hand.

My face was now on fire. I needed to quickly exit. "How about I bake up some samples and bring them by? You can choose a few you like to start with and we can go from there." Somehow I was able to carry on a sane conversation.

Joe stood and held out his hand. "I should get back to work," he said.

I shook his hand, holding it just slightly longer than socially acceptable for a platonic shake. *Oh boy.* "Thank you for your time. I'll be in touch." I touched Uncle Jack's arm and guided him outside. The fresh air hit my face for a reality check. I quickly took off toward the antique shop.

"Whoa there," Uncle Jack said, jogging to catch up to me. "I have to say, you're already getting in better shape."

I kept silent and tried to retain my brisk pace. If I did so, I might just keel over by the time we got back. I slowed down a notch. "I think that went well." I was grateful he pushed me outside my comfort zone, but I didn't want to say that to encourage him further.

"I agree. I think he likes you," Uncle Jack said.

I stopped, mostly for emphasis but also to catch my breath. "Uncle Jack. Do not go fixing me up. It will be a long time before I want to pursue a romantic interest."

He held up his hands. "OK. Message received. It might not be on my timeline, but Cupid has his own." He snickered and took off.

Oh boy. Well, I said my piece. We continued silently on our walk, Uncle Jack considerately slowing to match my pace.

"You just never know when the love bug will hit," he said. His tone implied he had something up his sleeve.

I didn't want to get into a disagreement with the man who had so lovingly taken me in during the worst time of my life. His heart was huge and always in the right place. Perhaps with fewer years left on the earth, he was becoming more of a romantic. I let his comment go by. He was quite insightful, but I more than had my hands full with the bakery.

As we neared the antique shop, he stopped and pointed to the end of the harbor. "Do you see the lighthouse?"

I looked in the direction he indicated. "Of course."

"The top level has been converted to a small, charming restaurant. Just perfect for two lovebirds," he said and sped off for the final distance to the shop.

"Uncle Jack!" I admonished and shook my head, following him.

Inside the store, he busied himself in the corner opposite the bakery.

I said to him, "Don't think I don't know what you're doing." We both smiled, and I bounced over to the kitchen to fill my cooled cupcakes with cream. This time, I would taste it to be sure it was the right stuff. Lesson learned. My mind wandered to Joe. I just couldn't let myself go there yet. But could I be disciplined to remain focused on my business? Time would tell. I smiled as I finished preparing the cupcakes. If I could spend every day like this, I would be in heaven.

CHAPTER ELEVEN

I stopped and looked in the small mirror that hung next to the door in my cottage. I pinched my cheeks, wanting to make sure this was all real. My life was nothing like it was just a few short months prior. I had my own adorable place to do just as I wanted. My eye for design had so far garnered me a bed, a small table and chair to eat at, a love seat, and a television. The TV had only been on a bit each morning as I got ready for work. I couldn't bring myself yet to just be in the quiet. My brain needed some background noise.

The stress lines around my eyes had noticeably diminished since I had moved to Belle Harbor. I chalked it up to the sea air. But spending time with one of my favorite people on the planet contributed significantly to my disposition. Today, I had to walk to the shop since the moped was still being repaired. I cherished the time to gather my thoughts along the way. They had settled down after Joe and I had made several pages of notes last night. My plan for our collaboration was coming together. If this was successful, I had even more ideas percolating about other business deals.

At this hour, the beach was sparsely dotted with the early risers. Experiencing life in a vacation venue had to put a positive spin on things. If it didn't, why would you live here?

The door to the store was open, and Uncle Jack and Justin were deep in conversation. "And speak of the devil." Uncle Jack lifted his head when he saw me enter. I ignored his comment.

"Hi guys." I waved. "You're here early, Justin." I slipped off my backpack and stood next to them.

"Yeah, I'm looking for that little rascal again. For the life of me, I can't figure out how he continues to escape," Justin said. He started weaving through the aisles, looking under tables. "I just hope he's not causing any trouble."

"He's welcome anytime after what he did finding those clues to Cal's death. Barney wouldn't say, but I got the feeling that may have broken the case wide open." Uncle Jack was a bit dramatic. I didn't see how a piece of a kite or some footprints in the dust could lead to anything. But a kite flier who was used to always winning? Would that be enough to make someone angry to kill the judge? I shuddered. It sounded like Cal may not be well liked with employees bad-mouthing him and his business. It did explain a bit about why my moped pooped out. I only hoped Uncle Jack hadn't wasted his money on a lemon.

"We can keep looking for him if you need to get to work," I offered.

Justin looked at Uncle Jack and back at me. He came around the table and stood next to us. "Nah, Justin makes his own hours," Uncle Jack said and winked at Justin. "That's how it is in the agriculture business."

Justin giggled. "Sure, Jack. But Tilly's right. I should be going. I'll stop in later to see if you've found my little guy." He headed to the door and almost collided with a customer rushing in.

The man's clothes were disheveled, and I suspected that he may be a homeless person. His wool plaid shirt was overdressed for the weather. His construction style pants were worn and dirty. He turned to see Justin leave and came further into the store. I pulled out my phone in case I needed to dial 9-1-1. Big city life had taught me well in situational awareness. The man reached into his pants pocket and pulled out something he gripped in his hand with a chain dangling. He looked at the open door again, and back at Uncle Jack.

"What do you have there?" Uncle Jack inquired.

The man looked at me, then around the room. "A watch. Do you buy these types of things?" he asked. He held his arm out, cupping the timepiece.

I took several steps toward the duo, my phone remaining at the ready.

"May I?" Uncle Jack asked.

The man looked at him and nodded. He carefully transferred the watch to my uncle. I could see an intricate design along with writing on the cover of the watch. Uncle Jack clicked it open and some type of red jewels sparkled from inside the watch. He gently closed it and handed it back to the man. He rubbed his chin. Pointing to the watch, he said, "That's a bit above my pay grade, but I have a lot of dealers that I can contact to see if they're interested."

The man jammed the watch back into his pants pocket. "I don't need to see a dealer. What could you give me for it?"

"Well." Uncle Jack crossed his arms. "The problem is if I buy it, I don't really have a clientele that could afford it."

The man took two steps toward the door. My instincts said Uncle Jack was slow-dancing this guy somewhere. "OK. When can you get in touch with the dealer? I'm kind of in a hurry."

"Give me a day or two. Just a sec." Uncle Jack turned and headed to the cash register.

The man's eyes darted around, scanning the other items on the tables.

Uncle Jack returned with pencil and paper. He handed it to the guy and said, "Write down your name and number, and I'll let you know when I have something for you."

The guy looked down and shook his head. "I'll come back. I need it soon, though. My mother is sick and she needs the money for her treatment." He turned and almost ran from the store.

"Uncle Jack," I said.

"Don't worry, Tilly. I've been doing this long enough. That's the exact watch the woman was looking for the other day." I followed him back to the cash register. "There's obviously something fishy between the both of them."

He picked up the phone, dialed, and grinned. I think he was maintaining calm more for my sake. My heart raced just as if the guy had come to rob us with a gun. This was not the life I had envisioned in a happy, little beachside town.

"Yeah. Barney. Jack. Got a lead on that watch. Guy just came in with it. I put him off, but I'm sure it won't be for long. He wants to dump it ASAP." Uncle Jack nodded. "All right. See you soon." He hung up the phone and rubbed his hands together. "We're going to nail that jerk. Nothing much peeves me more than people stealing. Well, that and murder." He gestured to the wall we shared with the bookstore. "I got a feeling Barney is going to make an arrest soon."

It wouldn't be soon enough for me. The not knowing was hard. From my perspective, the crime against Cal was personal. That gave me the smallest amount of solace that I wasn't in danger. But if someone killed once, would they do it again? And this sketchy watch gave me concern for Uncle Jack. If he did this guy wrong, no telling what people desperate for money would do.

CHAPTER TWELVE

I headed back to the kitchen and my happy place. Cupcakes never stole or murdered. The worst thing they did was add to my weight, and I'd take that risk all day long over fear for my life. I got the bowl of cream from the refrigerator and spooned it into a pastry bag. I squeezed a dollop onto my finger and tasted it, just in case. I closed my eyes and swallowed it. Mmm. Sweetness. I lined up the cupcakes on the counter and started at the left end, poking a hole in each cupcake and squeezing it full of filling. I continued on until I had the two dozen cupcakes filled and ready for the icing. I had made a batch of chocolate ganache to top them off. Never too much chocolate in my book.

"Hey there," I heard Uncle Jack call out as Barney arrived. Our little town police chief seemed to be a regular at the antique shop. Never mind that he and Uncle Jack were old friends and poker buddies. This had to be the most excitement in Belle Harbor in quite some time. "Thanks for coming so quickly. You know, my memory for details ain't what it used to be." He chuckled.

"What are you thinking, Jack? Is the watch hot?" Barney asked. "Hi Tilly." He waved to me in the kitchen.

I waved back. "I'll have fresh cupcakes to sample in a bit."

"Barney, I don't know if you're more interested in the stolen watch or getting dibs on the cupcakes," Uncle Jack said. "I think Tilly's bakery is going to be good for my antique business too." He looked at me and smiled.

"That is, if we don't eat all of her profits." Barney chuckled.

Uncle Jack pulled out a piece of paper and handed it to Barney. He pointed at it. "Here's the watch the guy brought in. I found this online. Likely worth about twenty Gs."

Barney whistled and looked up. "I might be in the wrong business."

"Has anyone reported it missing? A woman was in here a few days ago looking for that same watch," Uncle Jack said.

Barney headed back to the kitchen, followed by Uncle Jack. They watched me frost the cupcakes. "Nope," Barney said. "I think I'd remember that. But there's a lot going on. That investigation into Cal's death is keeping me and my deputy pretty busy."

"What's the latest?" I asked.

He continued his observation of my work. "Well, for starters, we've interviewed the other judges in the kite competition. And with Cal's shady business dealings, there's a lot of people that appear to have a beef with him. It's more complicated than I expected."

I handed him a cupcake. There wasn't going to be any further progress on the investigation until he got one of these in his belly. He put almost half of it in his mouth, leaving a cream-covered mustache.

"Oh, for heaven's sake, Barney." Uncle Jack handed him a napkin. I handed my uncle a cupcake, and he followed suit, taking a huge bite.

I gave him a napkin. "I'm going to have to put a quota on you two."

Barney rolled his eyes. "These are just too good. One more? Then I promise I'm done. For now."

"OK." I slid one across the counter with another napkin. "But I need some left over to take next door."

Barney snapped his head up. "You mean to Flo?"

"Don't let her hear you refer to her that way. She made it clear that it's Florence," I said. I finished icing the last cupcakes and began loading a dozen of them into a box for delivery.

"Of course," Barney said, wiping his salt-and-pepper mustache again for good measure. "Do you know what her situation is?" He looked back and forth between Uncle Jack and me.

"Barney, you old devil," Uncle Jack said. "Don't tell me you're smitten with her?" He reached for another cupcake, and I tapped his hand and shook my finger at him.

"Smitten? What are you? Out of the 1920s?" Barney replied. "I'm just asking. I didn't see a ring on her finger."

"Well, maybe you haven't lost your investigative skills after all," Uncle Jack said. "That's very observant of you."

Barney headed back to the front of the store and started mindlessly picking through items on the tables, picking up an antique schooner and holding it up high. "Maybe I'll buy this. I have just the perfect spot for it," he said.

"Don't try to dodge the subject, my friend." Uncle Jack followed him. "Spill it," he said.

"She seems nice enough. And I like to read. So I think we would have something in common," Barney said, avoiding all eye contact, continuing to look the ship over from all angles. He moved to the cash register, set it on the counter, and got out his wallet. I didn't know if he really wanted that, but he was willing to spend money to get the subject changed.

"Barney. You old dog. Good for you," Uncle Jack said. He played along with Barney, took his money, and packaged up the ship to go. "I hope that looks just like you want it to in your house." Uncle Jack smirked.

Barney took a couple of steps in my direction. "Tilly, why don't we go out to celebrate you opening your business?"

"Oh, you don't have to do that. I haven't done much yet. Except make Uncle Jack sick with the first batch of cupcakes," I said.

Barney looked at Uncle Jack and back at me and grimaced.

"Don't worry. There was a mix-up in the cream filling. But as you tasted, that's all been corrected," I assured him.

He nodded. "Well, I think that's a success." He looked at Uncle Jack. "Why don't we take her to Fiona's? She could stand to meet someone her own age since she's just been hanging out with us two old codgers," Barney said.

"Hey, speak for yourself," Uncle Jack countered. I was convinced he didn't think of himself as old. And he certainly didn't act his age. "But yes, Fiona's would be great. And I think they would get along well."

"Now that you two have my social calendar filled, why don't we pay Florence a visit and deliver these cupcakes?" I asked.

I held out the box for Barney to take. He looked at Uncle Jack and said, "Not a word." He took the box, and we followed him out the door. For the life of me I couldn't see Florence as much more than an eccentric cat lady. But beauty was in the eye of the beholder. I tried to imagine Barney and Florence as an item, but my brain wouldn't go there. I hoped for Barney's sake that she didn't break his heart. He was a gem, too, and one of Uncle Jack's best friends. The two of them had been inseparable since Uncle Frank had passed. And I was grateful to Barney for that. Maybe I would whip up a batch of cupcakes just for him. We hadn't started off on the right foot with Florence, and I hoped the cupcakes would be a sufficient peace offering. And if she had any interest in Barney, his delivery of them would just sweeten the pot.

CHAPTER THIRTEEN

The appearance and ambiance of the bookstore had been transformed from the cluttered mess of moving day. Walls held shelves lined with nicely arranged books, nothing out of place. In between the shelves were overstuffed chairs with ottomans and side tables holding rustic lamps. Each little nook looked like a cozy reading corner where you could cuddle up and spend hours with a good book.

The center of the room was dotted with small round tables holding books on display. The tea corner in the back of the room still looked ready to host the first gathering.

Barney led the welcoming committee boldly into the store. Florence had her head in a box and looked up as we approached. Barney held the box of cupcakes in outstretched arms to show that we came in peace. She looked from Barney to Uncle Jack and me and back to Barney. She raised up and asked, "Can I help you?"

Barney forged ahead. "We brought you a welcome to the neighborhood gift. Actually, Tilly made them." He flicked his head in my direction. "You get to taste the most delectable treat you've ever had."

Florence accepted the box and set it on the counter. That woman still had her game face on. I didn't know what it would take to get her to crack a smile. "Thank you."

"Maybe you could serve them with the tea," Barney suggested as he looked at the tea set up in the corner.

"No, we'll have the traditional biscuits with our tea." Florence returned to unpacking the box in front of her.

I felt like we were being dismissed. I turned to leave, making eye contact with Uncle Jack. He nodded his agreement at the sentiment.

"I love *The Great Gatsby*," Barney exclaimed.

Florence swung her head up from the box. "You do?" She stepped from behind the counter and picked up the book that was displayed on a stand at a nearby table. She thumbed through it, looking at Barney as if to assess his sincerity.

Barney took a step back, his face flushed. He rubbed his hands together. "Sure do. I enjoy many of the classics."

Florence joined us in the center of the room. Gwinnie sidled up to her, rubbing her leg and purring. Florence scooped her up in her free hand. "Maybe you would be interested in joining a book club. We'll have a new one every month," she said softly.

"Yes, I would," Barney said. He took a step closer to Florence. "Look, I'm really sorry for how things started here. We've almost finished our investigation into Cal's murder."

I looked at Uncle Jack, who shrugged. As far as we were aware, there was progress with clues and suspects, but Barney made it sound like an arrest was imminent. My money was on the disgruntled kite flier. When ego and money combined, many times it led to no good. But in this case, the end result was dire.

Florence looked down and returned the book to the display. She stroked Gwinnie, whose purr was now the loudest sound in the room.

Florence looked up at Barney, her demeanor returning to a more serious tone.

Barney continued, "You don't have anything to worry about. It wasn't a random crime. I'm certain you're safe here." He reached to pet Gwinnie, who resoundingly hissed at him.

"Oh, Gwinnie. Be nice to the man," Florence said. "She's just shy. I'm sure in due time she'll come around." The tips of Florence's mouth hinted at a smile. *Well, I'll be.* Barney was our secret weapon to crack the hard shell of Florence. Who knew? Florence's disposition returned to a serious tone. "I just can't get the sight of him out of my mind. I mean, the way he was laying there. Not moving." Her hand covered her mouth.

Barney approached Florence and stood on the opposite side from where she held Gwinnie, his hand on her back. "That must have been horrible for you."

Florence nodded. She put her hand over Gwinnie's eyes, as if reliving the scene. "And for Gwinnie."

Barney attempted another pet of Gwinnie, tentatively reaching his hand behind the cat's back. He gave two small strokes as a trial run. "She really saved the day. Without her and Willie finding the pieces of the kite in here, we might not be as far down the road on the investigation as we are."

Barney was laying it on thick. But Florence was eating it up. I was going to be curious how this relationship developed—if it did. All signs right now pointed to a little spark being ignited. Maybe that would spur Uncle Jack on to finding a love. I worried about his loneliness. I would be on the lookout for a suitable companion. Two could play at this matchmaking game.

"Well," Uncle Jack interjected. If either of us didn't interrupt, we might never get out of here. "We should probably get back to the antique shop. Barney? You coming?" Uncle Jack moved to the door and I followed him.

"I'd love to know how you like the cupcakes," I said to Florence.

Florence and Barney pivoted as if our presence had alarmed them. It was all I could do not to chuckle. Barney was likely in store for a lot of razzing from Uncle Jack.

I looked around Barney and said to Florence, "I would love the opportunity to provide the tea biscuits for your events." I held my breath, bracing for a bristled response. All she could say was no. And I was trying Uncle Jack's advice of taking action and putting myself out there before I was ready. I closed my eyes for a second.

"Hmmm" was Florence's response.

Well, that wasn't what I expected. I didn't know what to do with that response. "Please think about it and let me know. I'm happy to bring you a sample if you'd like," I offered.

"Thank you for the welcome cupcakes," Florence said to Barney. He opened his mouth, closed it, and smiled. "And come back again to get signed up for the book club. We're going to start soon. I'm really looking forward to bringing some culture to this place." Florence swept her arm in a half-circle, implying the town could use highbrow activities. She followed the three of us out the door. From the sidewalk, I peered through the window of the bookstore to see Florence smiling big. She turned and swayed back to the box she had been unpacking when we arrived. We might just end up being friendly business neighbors after all.

CHAPTER FOURTEEN

It was more of a brisk morning than I expected on my walk to the moped store. My ride had been repaired and was ready to be picked up. The coolness of the air did wonders to clear my head. With my latest batch of cupcakes, my confidence was increasing in my baking skills. I was proud of myself, so boldly offering to provide the tea biscuits to Florence. No doubt she would be a tough customer. But it would make me work that much harder to ensure they were top quality.

I rounded the corner of the moped building to the wide-open beach. Seeing the expanse of the ocean always gave me perspective. My time here in Belle Harbor, while quite exciting in many ways I couldn't have predicted, was just what I needed at this point in my life. And I couldn't be happier to be here with Uncle Jack. I opened the door to the moped store, and Cooper lifted his head up from the paperwork on the counter.

I raised my arm and waved. "Hi Cooper. I'm here to pick up my moped."

He scanned the room, as if looking for someone or something. I followed his glance to see what he was looking at. Nobody else except me was inside the store. I stepped to the counter and pulled out my wallet. "How much do I owe you?"

He shook his head and held out his hand, again looking around. What was I missing? I couldn't figure out what he saw. "You don't owe anything," he said.

"Of course I do. You fixed the moped. That must cost something." I opened my wallet and got out my credit card.

"No. The amount of lemons Cal sold was staggering. Now that he's gone, we are trying to do right by the customers."

"Wow. OK." I slipped my credit card back into its slot. "That's very nice of you."

"It's the least we could do. And can you tell Jack that it looks like Anna might get her job back?" He reached behind the counter, pulled out a set of keys, and handed them to me. "She was only guilty of telling the truth. And thankfully, that helped to put a stop to those horrible business practices." He escorted me to the front of the store to the lineup of mopeds on the sidewalk.

"He'll be so happy to hear that." I took the helmet from Cooper, stepped onto the moped, and inserted the key. I looked at Cooper and turned the ignition. It fired right up. He gave me a thumbs-up and I rode away.

I had only ridden this thing a couple of times, but already I felt like I was getting the hang of it. Thankfully, it was just a short jaunt to the antique shop. Not many people were out yet. I decided last second to stop at Mocha Joe's, say hi, and pick up some coffee for Uncle Jack and myself. I slowly decelerated and pulled the moped to a gentle stop in front of the coffee shop. Uncle Jack's foresight to buy a moped with a basket on the back for deliveries was genius.

Mocha Joe and two other employees were behind the counter serving customers. I waited my turn, and when I arrived at the counter, Mocha Joe said, "Tilly! What a treat to see you. I'm ready for those pastries when you are. Let's do it." His exuberance gave me energy. I smiled at him, not sure if it was the caffeine or his natural positivity.

I laughed. "You got it. I'll be in touch soon. For now, just a couple of drip coffees to go."

Joe quickly grabbed two travel cups and pumped them full, placing lids over the steaming liquid.

I paid for them and asked, "Would you please also put them in a travel carrier?"

"Of course," he said and handed everything to me. "Tell Jack hello." He waved and moved over to help the next customer.

I carefully placed the coffee on the back of the moped and strapped the carrier into the basket. Crossing my fingers, I turned the key and it started right up again. Two for two. This was shaping up to be a great day. I sat tall on the seat and motored my way toward the antique store, visions of muffins in my head. I had just the recipe in mind that I wanted to try next for Mocha Joe's. Suddenly I realized I had come upon a person to my left that I didn't see until the last second. I swerved to miss her. The coffee from my basket flew, covering her entire right side.

She screamed, "Look what you've done. You idiot! Watch where you're going."

I stopped the moped and pushed it up against the building. "I'm so sorry. Here, let's go into my uncle's store. I've got some towels I can use to dry you off."

She looked up, and I recognized the woman from the other day who had come to Checkered Past Antiques looking for her stolen watch. The same watch that guy had come to sell a few days afterward. She brushed off her clothes, trying to remove the brown liquid. She scowled at me with daggers in her eyes. I hoped I hadn't just cost Uncle Jack a customer. And my day had started off so well.

She followed me into the store. I stopped when I got in the door, not expecting the scene I witnessed. Uncle Jack was there with Barney and the guy from the other day with the expensive pocket watch in handcuffs.

"What?" was all I could get out. I looked at Uncle Jack for an explanation.

He looked at me and then at the woman behind me, dripping with coffee. He tilted his head and furrowed his bushy brows.

"I had a little accident. I'm going to get some towels to help her clean up." I turned and looked at the woman again. "I'm so sorry." I headed back to the kitchen.

Uncle Jack stepped to the door, blocking the entrance. "You're just in time," he said.

I turned around, confused by his statement. "In time for what?" I asked, then realized he wasn't talking to me.

Barney stepped forward and began with the Miranda rights, "You are under arrest for the murder of Cal Borman. You have the right..." He turned the woman around and cuffed her.

She tipped her head down. "This isn't fair. If that loser hadn't sold me a lemon, it wouldn't have broken down. And my precious watch that was supposed to fund my retirement wouldn't have been stolen by that lowlife when I had to go for help." She sobbed into her chest.

My eyes bulged as I looked at Uncle Jack for answers. Was this the conclusion to Cal's murder? Were we safe now? Why would someone commit murder for a stolen watch?

The door opened again, and Barney's deputy arrived. He nodded one time toward Barney, silently acknowledging the plan. The deputy held the woman by her left elbow, and Barney took the man as they escorted them from the shop.

I moved toward Uncle Jack. "I don't understand."

He chuckled. "Barney put two and two together about the watch and traced it back to the woman. As soon as the guy came back to sell the watch, he had me call the woman to come get it. I had no idea his plan was two birds with one stone."

I put my hand on Uncle Jack's arm. That was a lot of drama for one morning. "Are you OK?"

"Are you kidding? We just nabbed a thief and a killer. I'm on top of the world. Now"—he started toward the back of the store—"we just need to get your business off the ground."

I stood where I was. "How can you be so calm about that?" My heart continued to race. I was pretty sure with my adrenaline level I could outrun anyone at this point.

"Ah, pish. Just another day at the office." Uncle Jack started arranging a table of antiques. It was starting to look a little more orderly after all.

I didn't understand how he could be so nonchalant about it. But I tried to follow his lead. Next up on my list for baking was the healthy muffin recipe. I only hoped I wasn't in for cardboard flavor with this flax and bran combo. Getting back to some baking would calm my nerves.

CHAPTER FIFTEEN

The music thumped in the background as the hostess led us to a booth. Fiona's was a bar that, from the looks of it, was a popular watering hole. Barney, Uncle Jack, and I took our seats as the hostess placed waters, drink coasters, and menus on table. The back wall illuminated a large display of liquor bottles. Three televisions hung above the display, showing various sporting events. Customers filled the horseshoe-shaped bar. A younger woman wearing a baseball cap serving drinks waved at our table. Barney and Uncle Jack returned the gesture.

"This place has great energy," I said, picking up a menu. And many good bar food choices. A lot of comfort food. Just what I needed.

"Wait 'til you meet Fiona," Uncle Jack said, smirking. I wondered what I was in store for this time. He seemed to want me to experience more adventure. Truthfully, I was ready for a little dullness after everything that had happened since I arrived in Belle Harbor.

"What's good here?" I asked, running my finger along the choices on the menu.

Barney looked at me. "You can't go wrong with a burger."

"No, you can't. Hi guys. And you must be Tilly." The woman reached across the table to shake my hand. "I've been looking forward to meeting you," she said. "And what took you guys so long to get in here?" She play-punched Barney in the arm.

"Fiona, we've been a little busy," Uncle Jack said.

"I've heard! Why don't I get you started with a round on the house of our specialty paloma cocktail?" She looked at each of us as we nodded. Fiona left to fill our order.

"I can see why the place has energy. She's great," I said, taking a sip of water.

"I'm glad you think so. I thought you two might hit it off. And you can finally have someone your own age to hang out with instead of us old geezers." Uncle Jack tipped his head back and laughed. It was good to see him relax for a bit.

"Hey!" Barney said. "Speak for yourself." Those two had such great banter.

"Yeah, I guess. You did mastermind the takedown of those two the other day," Uncle Jack said. "Spill the beans, how did you know who killed Cal?"

Barney took a long swig of his water, for what seemed like a dramatic pause. "Well, first, everything made it look like Maverick had done it. Motive was a bit weak, but sometimes it's the smallest thing that's the final straw that sends someone over the edge."

Fiona brought our drinks and placed them in front of us. The pinkish-colored drink in a highball glass bubbled. "Here you go," she said. "Stacy will be here in a jiffy to get your orders. Enjoy."

I took a sip of the refreshing cocktail. It was a nice, smooth combination of tart and sweet. The woman knew her stuff.

Barney continued, "It just didn't sit right with me. I've known that kid since he was little. He's got a temper, and no doubt he's competitive, but I couldn't envision him as a killer."

I held my drink glass close to me, nursing it to the bottom.

"I can see that, now that you say it. But how in the world did you ever trace things back to the woman?" Uncle Jack asked. I looked over at his glass, and the drink was gone. If we didn't pace ourselves, Fiona would have to wheel us out of here.

"I took a step back and looked at Cal's life. It didn't take me long to see that his businesses were a huge source of conflict for many. His customers and employees."

"Ah, yes. Anna. I'm glad you're the one who has to connect the dots. I couldn't do your job." Uncle Jack held his arm up, signaling Fiona for another round.

"I do love me a good puzzle. Once I started digging into his recent business transactions and looking at each customer, a pattern began to emerge. I'm actually surprised something hadn't happened to him sooner as despicable as he was. Not that getting scammed in a business deal is any reason to murder someone."

Uncle Jack nodded. "Life's too short to get that upset about things."

Stacy arrived with our second round of drinks and took our order, burgers all around.

"I put my usual chart together on the board with the victim and suspects. When I noted a motive for each one, the strongest driver came from the woman he sold a lemon to. It wasn't her first car from Cal."

"But a lot of people bought lemons, like me and Tilly. We didn't take it out on Cal by killing him," Uncle Jack said.

I tipped my glass up and finished my first round. I was beginning to feel the effects of the liquor and relaxed a bit.

"Right. But once you follow the money, a couple of people popped up to the top of the list. And the final piece is when you called about a guy trying to fence that stolen watch."

Uncle Jack shook his head. "You're hurting my brain with all of that." He laughed.

Fiona arrived with our burgers piled high next to a mound of fries. My eyes were bigger than my stomach. But I was going to attempt finishing the entire thing.

"Hey, Tilly. We've got a tasting night coming up at the bar. Why don't you come?" Fiona asked.

"That's what I'm talking about," Uncle Jack said. "A girl's night out."

I looked at Fiona and said, "I'd love to. Thank you."

"Great!" She squealed and clapped her hands. "You two are welcome to come too." She pointed to Uncle Jack and Barney.

They both shook their heads in unison and said, "No way."

"Ah, we're not that wild," Fiona said. "Maybe I should host a senior night just for you two."

Uncle Jack and Barney looked at each other wide-eyed. "Really?"

Fiona laughed. "Well, I was joking. But maybe it's not that crazy of an idea after all." She looked over her shoulder at the growing crowd. "Gotta go. Tilly, I'll be in touch. You two"—she pointed at Barney and Uncle Jack—"stay out of trouble."

"Well, that's not gonna happen," Uncle Jack said. I had no doubt he meant it. My life in Belle Harbor was not what I expected. But it was just what I needed.

WHAT'S NEXT? MUFFINS AND MISDEEDS

A mysterious letter from the past, gut punching muffins, and funky smelling clues...

Second in the Belle Harbor Cozy Mystery series!

Tilly is settling into her new cottage and life in the quaint beach town of Belle Harbor. With her fledgling bakery partnering with the local coffee shop, she has high hopes that her business will soon take off.

Tilly's new friend Fiona convinces her to rummage through her uncle's antique shop to find decor to fill her sparse home. But instead of the sought after beach treasures, they discover clues to a long ago unsolved mystery in the small town.

Coupled with the recent murder of a distillery owner, their investigation into the ancient family feud reveals shocking lies, sabotage, and the ultimate revenge. As they get deeper into the town's historical secrets, they discover a stink they can't ignore. Can Tilly's budding friendship bloom into a dynamic duo of crime solvers in time to save her new friend from going to jail?

Get Muffins and Misdeeds from Amazon and start reading right away!

SNEAK PEEK OF MUFFINS AND MISDEEDS

"Tilly, so sorry I'm late," he said.

I looked at my watch. "Actually, you're right on time." I stood and met him.

Justin's brow beaded with moisture. He appeared as anxious as I felt. Well, at least we were in this together.

"Are you OK?" I asked. He was not normally this jittery. Not that I had a lot of firsthand knowledge. But he generally exuded the calmness of the sea.

Justin fiddled with his wallet, turning it over in his hands. "Sure. I was just rushing to get here so you didn't have to wait long." He stepped forward to the rental shack to secure us a kayak.

I pulled money out of my pocket and extended my hand. "Here's my share," I said.

He looked at me and smiled. "Nah, I got this. You can get the next one." He paid the attendant, who pointed to a red kayak at the end of the row. Justin put his wallet away. "Weather cooperated. That's cool," he said.

We headed to our kayak. "Is it ever not this nice in Belle Harbor?" I asked.

"We do have an occasional storm. But overall, the weather doesn't stray far from how it is today," he said. We arrived at the kayak, and Justin removed the paddles and set them to the side. He pushed it about one-third of the way into the water. "Why don't you get in first? Then I'll shove us off and jump in."

I stepped into the kayak with my left leg, facing the shore. He steadied it and my right leg followed. I sat back, waiting for Justin to enter.

He moved to the bow and grabbed the handle. After lifting one end he moved it a bit further into the water. Any more and he would get wet before he could get in. He looked up at me, his sideburns dripping. Hopefully a relaxing trip on the water would allow him to cool off. He picked up the kayak and shoved off to begin our float without jumping in. With outstretched arms, his eyes widened. Unable to stop the momentum of the kayak, he let it go. I drifted farther from the shore. By myself. With no paddles.

Get Muffins and Misdeeds from Amazon and start reading right away!

WHAT'S AFTER MUFFINS AND MISDEEDS?

Birthday Cake and Burglary

Scrumptious sprinkle cake, bookstore chickens, and seeing double...

Third in the Belle Harbor Cozy Mystery series!

Tilly Griffin is on top of the world. With her newfound freedom in quaint Belle Harbor she is learning to love life again. Her plans for an epic birthday bash for her cherished and kooky Uncle Jack are almost complete.

Tilly's joy and whimsy soon turn to horror as she discovers the death of Poppy, a beloved local business owner. Rumors swirl about likely culprits that put the coming annual Arts Walk, which brings millions to the town coffers, in jeopardy.

As Tilly collects clues in the suspicious death, she learns of scandalous schemes, petty people, blackmailing busybodies, and snobby store owners, all who have a reason to want Poppy dead. Can Tilly put the pieces together in time to catch the killer and save the Arts Walk or will she be forced to pack up and find a new place to call home?

Get Birthday Cake and Burglary from Amazon and start reading right away!

MORE FROM SUE HOLLOWELL

Book 4 - Sugar Cookies and Scandal

A mysterious collection of books, estate sale discoveries, and growing family drama ...

Relations between Tilly, Uncle Jack and the antique shop's bookstore neighbor were finally moving the right direction. That is, until a surprise addition arrives in town, putting them all in an awkward situation.

As Tilly tries to unravel the new dynamic, matters are complicated by the death of the local veterinarian's assistant. With no time to spare for being the peacemaker, Tilly is on the hunt for a new location for her growing bakery business. Her recent inclusion of catering to her services sends her on the search for an assistant.

No sooner does she find the perfect match, than the suspect list for the murder takes a turn for the worse. As the cast of characters quickly grows to include several animals, Tilly wonders who among the barnyard culprits could have committed the dastardly deed. Can she solve the murder before it's too late? Or will the chickens finally come home to roost?

Book 5 - Tiramisu and Turmoil

A catering calamity, pesky paparazzi, and a celebrity wedding whodunit...

With Tilly's new assistant on board at the bakery, she agrees to take on a catering gig that could skyrocket her business to the next level. While jousting for her space in the kitchen with the temperamental chef, a troubling discovery at the celebrity wedding of the century threatens to shatter her dreams.

Joined by her bestie and armed with enough mascarpone for a lifetime supply of cheesecakes, Tilly sets out to solve the murder. She soon learns why the actors in attendance have won Academy Awards. Nothing is as it seems.

As Tilly quickly discovers, family drama and professional jealousy disguise the clues, making it a doozy of a mystery to detect what's real and what's fake. Will the publicity from the event doom the next phase of her bakery plans, or will Tilly be able to uncover the truth in a humdinger of a plot?

Book 6 - Pies and Pandemonium

A pie to die for, tangled family ties, and farmer's market folly...

Buoyed by a new baking alliance with her business neighbor, Tilly teams up with her to enter the annual berry pie competition. Coupled with her parents first visit to quaint Belle Harbor, Tilly's got her plate full. No sooner does she reconnect with her mom, than a dead body inserts itself front and center.

With the death of his father, the heir apparent to the ceramic pie plate empire is prime suspect number one. But as Tilly, and her unlikely sleuthing partner mom team up to investigate, they quickly find layers of deception buried deep in the history of the annual pie competition.

Tilly and her mom reveal the length contestants will go to for the top prize in the contest. Can they slice up this juicy mystery to serve up the killer or will they be forced to eat humble pie?

Book 7 - Coffee Cake and Calamites

A mysteriously disappearing body, tipsy travelers, and the clickety-clack of steel wheels...

Tilly, her uncle, and their friends are escaping for a short getaway on the Coast Excursion train. Romance is in the air with Tilly's uncle and her new assistant. As the train begins its journey to the vineyard, Tilly soon overhears whispers among the other guests about plans to dispose of a body.

Matters are further complicated as several of the guests over indulge at the wine tasting, returning to the train with even bigger tales of intrigue. When some of them are noticeably absent after the stop at the mystery mansion, Tilly is concerned whether she, her uncle and friends will all make it back to Belle Harbor alive.

Can Tilly find out the truth of the dead body and nab the suspect before the trip is over? Or will the killer escape from the ride, getting away with murder?

CREAM-FILLED CUPCAKES RECIPE

T illy's Cream filled cupcakes with Ganache frosting

CUPCAKES:

2 cups sugar

1 cup 2% milk

1 cup canola oil

1 cup water

2 large eggs, room temperature

1 teaspoon vanilla extract

3 cups all-purpose flour

1/3 cup baking cocoa

2 teaspoons baking soda

1 teaspoon salt

FILLING:

1/4 cup butter, softened

1/4 cup shortening

2 cups confectioners' sugar

3 tablespoons 2% milk

1 teaspoon vanilla extract

Pinch salt

DIRECTIONS

In a large bowl, beat sugar, milk, oil, water, eggs and vanilla until well blended. Combine flour, cocoa, baking soda and salt; gradually beat into egg mixture until blended.

Fill paper-lined muffin cups halfway. Bake at 375° until a toothpick inserted in the center comes out clean, 15-20 minutes. Remove from pans to wire racks to cool completely.

In a small bowl, beat butter, shortening, confectioners' sugar, milk, vanilla and salt until fluffy, about 5 minutes. Insert a very small tip into a pastry bag; fill with cream filling. Push tip through bottom of paper liner to fill each cupcake. Frost cupcakes.

GANACHE FROSTING:
1 cup semisweet chocolate chips
3/4 cup heavy whipping cream

Place chocolate chips in a small bowl. In a small saucepan, bring cream just to a boil. Pour over chocolate; whisk until smooth. Cool, stirring occasionally, to room temperature or until ganache reaches a dipping consistency.

Dip cupcake tops in ganache; chill for 20 minutes or until set. Store in the refrigerator.

About The Author

Sue Hollowell is a wife and empty nester with a lot of mom left over. Finding a lot of time on her hands, and as a lover of mystery novels, she began telling the story of a character who appeared in her head.

The Chemical Bond is a book about Meredith, Markette, a young woman who reluctantly enters into the field of law enforcement when her police officer father is killed in the line of duty. Her quest is to discover his murderer and in the meantime come to terms with a tragedy of her youth.

Will this book ever see the light of day? Maybe. Sue really likes the story and character. And writing that book taught her a ton about the publishing industry. Through this experience she has discovered a love of writing stories, and especially mysteries. She hopes you enjoy her books as much as she enjoys writing them.

Connect with Sue on Facebook at www.facebook.com/suehollowellauthor and sign up for her newsletter to stay in touch with all things cozy!

Printed in Great Britain
by Amazon

21488895R00058